Grandpa Jack
Scarlet

The Loony Doubloon

Collect all six exciting adventures:

1: Swashbuckle School

2: The Impossible Island

3: The Matey M'Lad

4: Freda the Fearless

5: The Loony Doubloon

6: The Vague Vagabond

The Loony Doubloon

Original concept by Sarah McConnell
Written by Lucy Courtenay
Illustrations by Sarah McConnell

A division of Hachette Children's Books

Based on the picture book *Don't Mention Pirates* © 2006
Sarah McConnell

First published in Great Britain in 2009
by Hodder Children's Books

1

A Catalogue record for this book is available from the British Library

ISBN: 978 0 340 98916 6 (HB)
ISBN: 978 0 340 95971 8 (PB)

Printed and bound in Great Britain by Bookmarque Ltd, Croydon, Surrey

The paper used in this book by Hodder Children's Books is a natural recyclable product made from wood grown in sustainable forests. The manufacturing processes conform to the environmental regulations of the country of origin.
The hard coverboard is recycled.

Hodder Children's Books
a division of Hachette Children's Books
338 Euston Road, London NW1 3BH
An Hachette UK Company

www.hachette.co.uk

Contents

1. The Fishomatic 9
2. Fritz the Glitz 24
3. The King of Bling 38
4. Wet Feet 50
5. Wig, 'Tache and Trolley Dash 65
6. Rich at Last 79

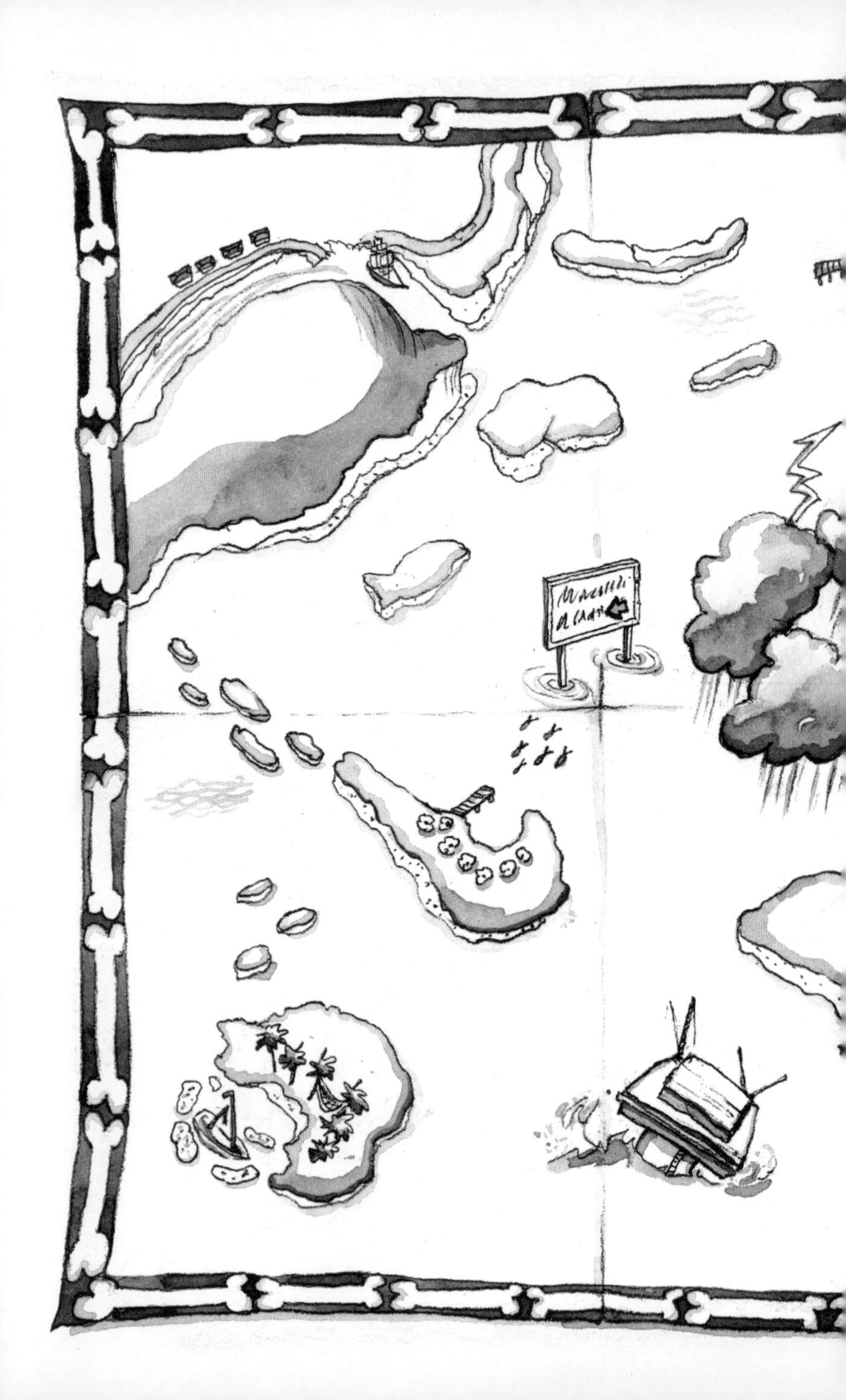

N

The Fishomatic

It was dawn aboard the world-famous pirate ship, *55 Ocean Drive.* A thick fog swirled between the masts and soaked the socks that had been left drying in the rigging the night before. Slugs had appeared from somewhere, eating the damp geraniums in the ship's window boxes. And a huge grey rock was looming out of the gloom.

"Rrrrrrock!" screeched a blue and

yellow budgie sitting up in the crow's nest overhead.

"Thanks, Bluebeard!" shouted Scarlet Silver, the small blonde pirate in a bright red pirate hat standing at the wheel. "All hands on deck!"

She slammed her hand on a button beside the ship's wheel.

There was a ringing noise below her feet, followed by a lot of clatter. Scarlet's crew fell up the cabin steps, through the cabin door and landed on the foggy deck in a heap.

Lipstick the parrot was pecking at the curlers in Scarlet's mum Lila's hair.

Scarlet's dad Melvin was twisting his straw-like moustache into shape, with Ralph the ship's cat tucked under his arm. Scarlet's brother Cedric was trying to wash his face, forgetting that he'd already put his space helmet on. Scarlet's Grandpa Jack was pulling on his favourite fish jumper. Grandpa Jack's best friend One-Eyed Scott's pyjamas were falling down.

The rock was getting closer. Another minute and *55 Ocean Drive* would be smashed to smithereens.

"Wake up, you snoozy snorkel-brains! Hard a-starboard!" yelled Scarlet.

Everyone grabbed the wheel with Scarlet and heaved with their combined weight. The wheel whizzed to the right. The ship shuddered and turned, missing the rock by a catfish's whiskers.

Scarlet got back on to her feet. She flipped her beaded plaits over her shoulders. "About time you lot showed up," she said.

"That rock should have been red like your hat," said Lila. One of her curlers fell out and rolled down the deck. Ralph chased it. "How are you supposed to see grey rocks on a grey sea in the middle of a grey fog?"

"Sea rocks are always grey, always large and always dangerous," Scarlet said. "It's just one of those annoying facts you need to learn if you're ever going to be a decent pirate. And Mum?"

"Yes, dear?"

"You forgot to bring the socks in," Scarlet said, glancing up at the rigging.

"Whoops," said Lila.

"This flipping fog makes my bones ache," growled One-Eyed Scott. "Are we still on course for Bottle Island, Cap'n?"

"Just about," said Scarlet proudly. She'd been captain of her own ship for several months, but the novelty hadn't worn off.

"Why's it called Bottle Island?" asked Melvin curiously.

"Coz it's shaped like a banana," said Scarlet, rolling her eyes.

Melvin frowned at the island on the map. "Looks more like a bottle to me," he said.

Scarlet sighed. Her family drove her mental sometimes.

"Will the fourth puzzle piece be there, Scarlet?" Cedric asked. "Will we find Granny's tremendous treasure this time?"

Scarlet looked down at the strange square pendant around her neck. It was made of green enamel, with three blue enamel corners. The fourth corner – the last piece of the puzzle they were trying to solve – was missing.

"Underwater, overboard!" Lipstick squawked as soon as he saw the pendant. "Up on high and wave the sword! Solve the riddle at your leisure, come and find tremendous treasure!"

The bit about waving swords in Granny's riddle had always worried Scarlet. It was the only part of the rhyme they hadn't solved yet, and it was getting harder to ignore.

"In answer to both your questions, Cedric," Scarlet said, "maybe. But first, there's something urgent we have to do."

"More urgent than finding treasure?" said Lila, sounding shocked.

Scarlet nodded. "We need a new dinghy," she said.

Everyone started giggling. One-Eyed Scott whooped and slapped his bony knees with a roar.

"I can still picture that villain Gilbert Gauntlet's face when we set him adrift in our little boat," Melvin chortled.

"He was madder than a monkfish with the mumps," hooted Grandpa Jack.

"I'm glad we set him adrift," said Scarlet, "but a captain should *never* let her ship sail for too long without a dinghy. Just look at what happened to the *Titanic.*"

"Will we be able to buy a dinghy on Banana Island?" asked Lila.

"It's *Bottle* Island, Mum," Scarlet said patiently. "I was joking when I— look, never mind. Yes, I'm sure we'll find a dinghy there. But we'll have to watch out. Whenever we go ashore, Gilbert Gauntlet turns up. And if he was mad at us before, he'll be *seriously* mad now."

"Rancid raspberries," One-Eyed Scott grumbled.

"So," said Scarlet. "Any ideas on how to make some cash? Dinghies are expensive."

"Fishing," said Grandpa Jack. With Grandpa Jack, fishing was usually the answer.

"Belly dancing," suggested Lila.

"Building a rocket and flying to the moon," Cedric said.

Scarlet frowned at her little brother. "How would that make money?" she asked curiously.

"Dunno," said Cedric. "But it would be *great*."

"Fishing," Grandpa Jack insisted. "Honest, Scarlet. Me and Scott have been working on something that could make us a mint. Scotty?"

One-Eyed Scott hurried over to a corner of the deck, where something was huddling underneath a large yellow sailcloth. He pulled off the cloth with a flourish. Everyone stared at the weird contraption.

"What," said Melvin, "is *that*?"

"The Fishomatic," Grandpa Jack explained. "Our flying-fish fishing machine. They zoom over our deck every day, and we've never been able to catch 'em. But with this little beauty, we'll catch a million!"

A silver-winged fish suddenly soared over everyone's heads, straight into one of the nets on the Fishomatic. It landed with a slither and a splash in the huge bucket of water underneath. Everyone clapped. The Fishomatic *was* pretty impressive.

"Land ahoy!" Melvin shouted suddenly.

A rocky row of cliffs had popped on to the horizon.

"We'll hide the ship just in case Gilbert Gauntlet shows up," Scarlet decided. "We don't want him to see *us* before we see *him*. Right?"

As they sailed towards Bottle Island,

Grandpa Jack and One-Eyed Scott moved their Fishomatic to the middle of the deck. Before you could dance half a hornpipe, the Fishomatic was full of surprised-looking fish who'd never expected a net in mid-air.

Cedric spotted the cave first. The way Bottle Island's cliffs stood, it was nearly impossible to see the opening unless you were under one metre twenty. Luckily, Cedric was one metre ten. They guided *55 Ocean Drive* into the cave and dropped anchor with an echoey splosh.

"Good timing, Scarlet," said Grandpa Jack, patting the Fishomatic. "Any more fish and she'd have exploded."

"According to my chart, Bottle Island's harbour – Port Label – is that way," said Scarlet, pointing out of the cave.

"Without our dinghy, we'll have to swim for it."

Grandpa Jack and One-Eyed Scott netted all the fish and jumped into the water with the net tied between them.

"Whee!" Grandpa Jack shouted as the fish surged forward, towing the two old pirates through the water at full speed. "Hold on to your patch, Scotty!"

Ralph the cat rode on Melvin's head, lifting his tail out of the water as Melvin paddled after Grandpa Jack and One-Eyed Scott. Lila followed, her accordion wrapped in its waterproof casing and strapped to her back. Swearing at the sleepy-looking bats on the cave roof, Lipstick and Bluebeard swooped overhead. Cedric fixed two flipper attachments to the splints he wore to help him walk. Then he took Scarlet's hand. They leaped off the ship. Cedric pulled Scarlet through the water so fast that they overtook Grandpa Jack and One-Eyed Scott at the harbour mouth and ploughed up half the beach.

They were ashore.

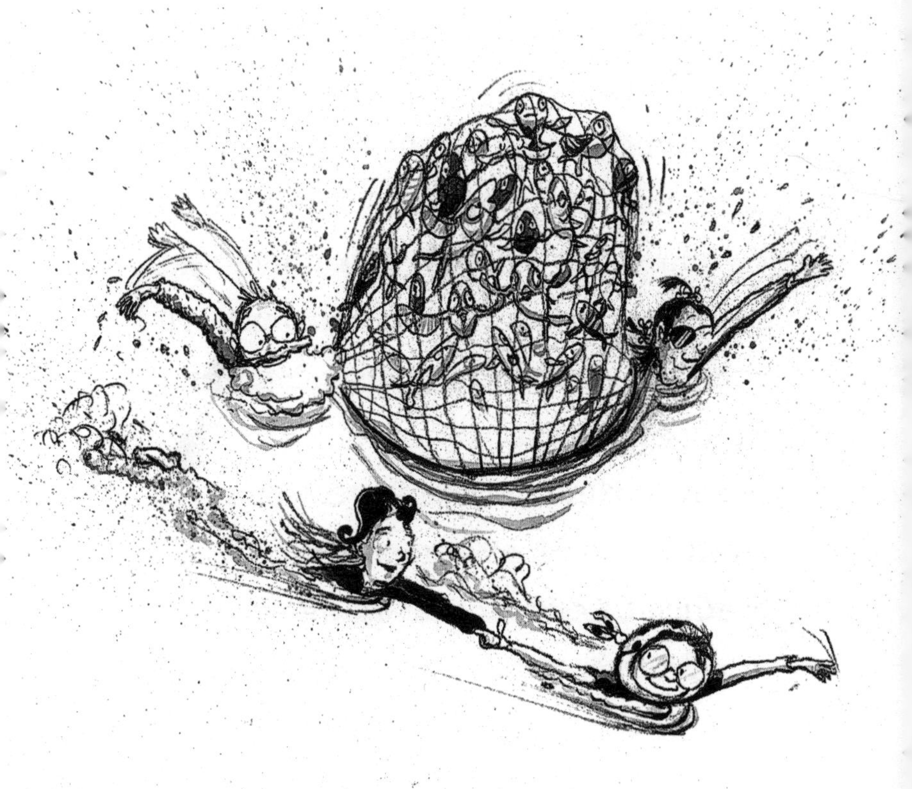

Fritz the Glitz

Port Label was very quiet. There were no ships in the harbour. No one was fishing, or shopping, or doing any of the things you expect to see in a seaside town. The only notable thing was the advertising all down the harbour front.

THE LOONY DOUBLOON! screamed the purple and gold hoardings. CRAZY PRICES! CRAZY DEALS! YOU'D BE CRAZY TO MISS IT!

"Gilbert Gauntlet," said Scarlet grimly.

Ralph hissed.

"Where?" Melvin gasped.

"Not *here*, Dad," said Scarlet. "There."

Gilbert Gauntlet beamed through the first "O" of LOONY DOUBLOON on the biggest hoarding of all. Scarlet half-expected her arch-enemy to rush around the corner waving a sword at her. *Wave the sword* ... Scarlet thought of Granny Joan's riddle. She wasn't old enough for swords, as her mother often reminded her. It was a worry.

"So what's the Loony Doubloon, then?" Lila wanted to know.

"One of Gilbert Gauntlet's scams, of course," said Scarlet, pushing the thought of swords to the back of her mind. "If the last three puzzle pieces are anything to go by, we'll have to beat him and help these islanders before we get hold of the fourth piece."

They walked down the harbour front. The houses that huddled beneath the hoardings were built out of something that sparkled in the sunlight.

One-Eyed Scott stared at the twinkling bricks. "Is them – gold ingots?" he asked.

"Fool's gold," Scarlet said. "Looks like gold, but isn't."

"I knowed that," One-Eyed Scott said. He looked embarrassed. Grandpa Jack sniggered.

"Best quality diamonds," said a bored-sounding voice. "Top-notch rubies. Goin' cheap today."

The Silvers turned to see a scruffy-looking treasure trader standing behind an even scruffier-looking treasure stall.

"Good prices," said the trader, fingering the bobble on his hat. "You won't buy diamonds no cheaper."

"This isn't a diamond," said Scarlet, picking up a sparkly pebble. "It's just a bit of glass."

The trader swelled up like a puffer fish. "It ain't!" he spluttered.

Cedric picked up a red stone labelled *rooby*. "And this isn't a ruby either," he said. "Anyone can see it's aluminium fused at a high temperature with a little chromium."

The trader slumped down on the chair behind his stall. "Bloomin' experts," he muttered. "That's all I need."

"Nice chair, though," said Lila kindly.

It was. Built out of driftwood, it was polished and beautifully carved.

"Cheers," sniffed the trader. "Made it meself. I do vehicles and vermin traps too. Hobby, like."

"I'm Scarlet Silver," said Scarlet. "And this is my family."

"Fritz is the name, Glitz is the game," said the trader, cheering up. "You want treasure? I can get treasure. Not this rubbish. The real deal. The bling. The ker'ching. The—"

"Actually," Lila interrupted, "we want a dinghy."

"No dinghies here," Fritz the Glitz said, shaking his head. "Just treasure. Bottle Island's famous for it. Rich too. Well, we was – before the Loony Doubloon took all our business away. Treasure superstore, see, up on the Bottleneck. Biggest in the Seven Seas. Now it's all we can do to feed our parrots."

"That *Gilbert Gauntlet,*" Lila said furiously. "If I ever meet his mother ..."

Fritz the Glitz looked horrified. "You *know* Gauntlet?"

"Oh yes," said Scarlet. "We know him. But we don't exactly send him Christmas cards. Listen – we really do need a dinghy. Would you maybe make one for us? Please?"

Fritz the Glitz stared at Scarlet like she was speaking Martian.

"I'm sure you'd be very good," Melvin said. "If your chair is anything to go by."

"Make a dinghy," Fritz the Glitz

muttered. He looked like someone had just whacked him around the head with a kipper. “Yeah. I could, right enough. Bit of wood, couple of nails, bit of varnish, pukka. How much?”

Grandpa Jack pointed at the large net of fish that he and One-Eyed Scott had dumped on the pavement. “This much,” he said.

Fritz the Glitz looked at the fish. He sucked his teeth in that special market-trader way. “A boat, yeah,” he said. “But you ain’t got enough fish for oars.”

“Me and Scotty could catch a few more fish to pay for the oars later,” Grandpa Jack told Scarlet.

“Deal,” said Fritz the Glitz. He spat on his hand and stuck it out. Scarlet spat on hers. They shook with a squelching sound.

Fritz the Glitz's wife ran out of the house and gawped at the silvery net on the pavement.

"Here, Mitzy!" Fritz said. "Some fellas here with some fish! They want me to make 'em a boat!"

Scarlet and her family left the Glitzes and walked on through Port Label. More tatty treasure stalls had sprung up, but there wasn't a single customer to be seen. No wonder the traders of Port Label all looked so miserable.

They approached a stall selling mounds of fake diamonds.

"Excuse me," said Melvin. "How do we get to the Loony Doubloon?"

The trader was a huge woman with a tiara perched on a nest of thick black hair. The sign above her stall said: Rhinestone Rhondda. She looked worried about losing the first customers she'd seen all week. "You don't want to go there," she said. "I'll do you a deal. I'll—"

"Don't worry," Scarlet interrupted. "We're not doing our shopping. We're out to stop Gilbert Gauntlet from cheating his way across the Seven Seas." She didn't mention the puzzle, or the tremendous treasure. It was all too complicated to explain.

Rhinestone Rhondda gasped. "But the Loony Doubloon is massive!" she said. "Gigantic! You might as well try to kill a giant squid with a matchstick!"

"You *can* kill a giant squid with a matchstick," Cedric told her. "It's all a matter of where you put the matchstick."

Rhinestone Rhondda shook her head, like she still couldn't believe what Scarlet was suggesting. "Town square," she said. "Shuttle bus. Don't really need it – you can walk. But folk like a bus ride. Specially when they've got shopping to carry."

In the town square, a queue of treasure shoppers were waiting at a large purple and gold bus shelter. LOONY DOUBLOON SHUTTLE BUS! screeched the hoarding above the bus stop. GO CRAZY TODAY!

A gold and purple double-decker

bendy-bus rolled into view, down the only road that Scarlet could see. It opened its doors with a rude farty noise. More than a hundred shoppers spilled out of the bus, clutching purple and gold shopping bags. A few pickpockets slunk out of the shadows and hovered around, looking hopeful.

"Shopping already, and only nine o'clock," Grandpa Jack said, shaking his head as he and the others climbed aboard the bus. "Ain't these folks ever heard of breakfast?"

As Rhinestone Rhondda had said, it wasn't a long trip. Leaning her head against the bus window, Scarlet listened to the excited chatter of the shoppers around her.

"... ever such a good deal on emeralds last week ..."

"... gold watches so heavy you gotta wear one on each wrist or you falls over ..."

"... hope they're still doing them silver toasting forks ..."

The view outside the window flattened and dipped. Scarlet could see the sea on both sides of the bus.

"Bottleneck," announced the spotty young pirate at the wheel. "All off here for the Loony Doubloon."

Scarlet stepped down on to the pavement and stared. Two hundred metres further down the road, an enormous structure swayed in the sea breezes gusting in from all sides. It twinkled. It flashed. Music spilled from the speakers hanging over the doors. The smell of precious metals wafted on the wind towards the bus stop.

"Loony, Loony, Loony Doubloon!" sang the speakers. "Trade your goods and trade 'em soon! Crazy deals both morn and noon! Loony, Loony, Loony Doubloon!"

The King of Bling

"Catchy," said Lila, tapping her toes as the speakers boomed away overhead.

"Mum!" Scarlet said crossly.

"This is loony all right," Melvin said, staring as the shoppers rushed for the golden trolleys that lined the road.

They entered the Loony Doubloon. It was impossible not to gasp. Treasure was piled high on all sides. There were vats of sparkling emeralds. Tubs of glinting sapphires. Gold and silver chains wrapped around bobbins the size of tractor wheels. Useful stuff, pointless stuff – sparkly stuff as far as the eye could see.

"*Adorable!*" said Lila, pouncing on a silk eyepatch sprinkled with tiny diamonds.

Melvin ran up to a huge golden piano, and Ralph plinked along its black and white diamond keyboard. Cedric spotted a family of aliens carved out of one enormous emerald. Grandpa Jack and One-Eyed Scott goggled at a pirate hook set with rubies, and Lipstick and Bluebeard found a pair of delicate filigree bird perches to swing on.

"Stay focused, crew," Scarlet said. Her eyes were watering from the golden glare. She took the aliens from Cedric

and put them back on the shelf. "We're here to beat Gilbert Gauntlet, find that last puzzle piece and get out of here."

The speakers started booming out that old pirate classic, *The Yo-Ho Hoedown*. There was a sudden scream of delight up by the tills.

"I'VE WON!"

An old man with a massive silver beard, woollen scarf, and silver hair peeping out from underneath an extraordinary hat, was dancing around and waving his till receipt. "I'VE WON!" he shouted again. "THE THOUSANDTH CUSTOMER! IT'S MEEEEE!"

"Lucky devil," sighed a nearby shopper with thick black dreadlocks snaking down her back.

"CongratulAAAAAYtions to our new

King of Bling!" came a booming voice over the speakers.

The shoppers cheered. The old man screamed with joy again.

"The King of Bling trolley dash is YOURS!" continued the voice. "You have one minute!"

The Silvers watched as the old man tore down the treasure-store aisles, grabbing all the gold and silver he could reach and piling it into his trolley.

"He moves fast for an old bloke," said One-Eyed Scott.

"Cod liver oil," said Grandpa Jack. "He must drink gallons."

"If you could get all that treasure for free," said the dreadlocked shopper with a sniff, "you'd run too."

"That whole trolley?" Cedric repeated.

He'd got hold of the emerald aliens again. Now he let them roll out of his hand. "For *free*?"

"I think we've seen enough," Scarlet said, looking grim.

"I'd just like to buy this teensy little eyepatch," Lila began, sidling towards the nearest queue. "So sweet, and relatively inexpensive. They only want a couple of silver pennies for it, and ..."

"Mum," said Scarlet, "we're leaving. RIGHT NOW."

She turned on the heels of her pink skull-and-crossbones boots and marched out of the store. Grumbling, the others followed. But then Scarlet stopped.

"The way out was *here*," she said, staring at a tower of gold ingots stacked to the ceiling like an expensive game of

Jenga. "I'm sure it was."

"It was that way," said Cedric, thumbing behind him.

"No!" Melvin and Lila shook their heads. "It was past the Pirate DVDs."

Ralph yawned, and patted the solid silver mouse he'd pinched from the Pampered Pets section across the floor as the others argued and walked around in circles. At last, they found a door, surrounded by large wooden crates. It looked like a back entrance.

They all heard the squeak of trolley wheels. Scarlet's pirate senses kicked in. She pushed her family behind one of the crates.

Around the corner came the old man from the

trolley dash. Then suddenly, he wasn't an old man any more. The silver beard and wig came off. Then the large silver eyebrows. The glasses were tucked into a pocket. The hunch straightened up, and the shabby brown coat was tossed into a corner. The vainest man on the Seven Seas adjusted his shining brown locks on his shoulders, fixed his moustache and checked on his bald patch with a tiny hand-held mirror.

The Loony Doubloon's King of Bling was none other than Gilbert Gauntlet's chief henchman, Captain Curl.

"What are we going to do?" Lila whispered hysterically.

Captain Curl slipped into a Loony Doubloon employee T-shirt and fiddled with his hair again.

"We're going to follow that preening prune and see what happens next," Scarlet said.

They tiptoed after Captain Curl as he pushed his treasure trolley slowly back into the store.

"So *that's* how Gauntlet can afford a trolley dash every thousandth customer," Melvin said as they watched the villain replacing the treasure on the superstore's shelves. "Curl puts it all back!"

"Captain Curl probably does the dash every time, disguised as someone else," said Cedric.

"So the real shoppers don't stand a chance!" Lila gasped.

One-Eyed Scott muttered something so rude about Gilbert Gauntlet's chief henchman that Ralph spat out his silver mouse and crept inside Melvin's jacket. Scarlet's pirate brain was whizzing. Now they knew how Gilbert Gauntlet tricked his customers, there had to be a way of turning the tables. She needed to work out a Plan.

Back in Port Label, the Silvers' new dinghy was taking shape. Fritz the Glitz had even started decorating the sides, chiselling out holes and studding them with fake diamonds.

"She's going to be a beauty," he said proudly. "Even if I sez so meself."

"Flying Fish Fricassee?" Fritz's wife Mitzy offered.

Scarlet's stomach rumbled. She realised they hadn't eaten anything since breakfast. There had been a selection of Loony Doubloon snacks for sale at the shuttle-bus stop on the way back to Port Label, but no one wanted to buy something that would put more money in Gilbert Gauntlet's pocket.

They all turned at the sound of splashing oars a little way offshore. A familiar voice came roaring over the choppy waves.

"I don't give a boiled beetroot for your blisters, Duncan! And I don't give a flying frog for your fingers, Derek! You're a bunch of snivelling snakes, the lot of you. Row, you stinkers – row! I need a bath, and a cup of tea. And I need them RIGHT NOW!"

Wet Feet

Scarlet threw herself down on the sand behind the new dinghy. The others did the same. Gilbert Gauntlet looked *furious.* The buttons on his pinstriped coat were crusty with salt. His lank hair hung around his ears and his black hat was covered in fish scales.

As soon as the rowing boat hit the sand, Gilbert Gauntlet squelched straight up to Mitzy in his waterlogged pirate boots. "Food," he said. "Now."

Trembling, Mitzy gave the pirate a bowl of fricassee. Gilbert Gauntlet ate the lot.

"Disgusting," he snarled, thrusting the bowl back at Mitzy. "You expect me to *pay* for that? I think not. TAXI!"

"No taxis here, Mr Gauntlet sir," Fritz the Glitz mumbled. "Just a bus."

For the first time, Gilbert Gauntlet noticed the Loony Doubloon hoardings along the seafront. "Ah!" he said, his face clearing. "Bottle Island, eh? I wondered where those rowing ruffians had brought me. Good, good. The penthouse above the Loony Doubloon will have everything I need. Derek? Desmond? Duncan? Doris?"

"It's *Dennis,* sir," said the thinnest of the four wet and shivering henchmen.

"Good gracious man, does it matter?" Gilbert Gauntlet demanded. He twitched his damp lace cuff. "Get along and catch that bus for me. Clear away the little people. They can wait for the next one. *Blasted* seawater. My silver cufflinks are *ruined.*"

"He's madder than Ralph with knots in his whiskers," One-Eyed Scott said as they watched Gilbert Gauntlet stride up the beach with his henchmen.

"Hey!" said Scarlet, realising something. "Our dinghy!"

The Silvers and One-Eyed Scott ran

across the sand to *55 Ocean Drive's* empty old dinghy. They stopped as if they'd run into an invisible wall.

"Phew," said Melvin, waving his hand in front of his face.

The dinghy smelt of rotten fish and crusty socks. Everyone backed away apart from Ralph. Bluebeard wafted his wings helpfully underneath Scarlet's nose.

"Just as well Fritz the Glitz is making us a new dinghy," said Scarlet as Ralph licked the prow of the stinky boat like it was a lollipop. "This one is ruined. Now, listen up crew. I have a Plan."

Everyone looked alert. Ralph stopped licking.

"Cedric?" Scarlet said. "How good is your maths?"

Cedric pulled up his trousers and flipped something on his left-foot splint. An abacus attachment popped out to the side. The little beads rattled in the breeze. "Ask the question, Scarlet," he said.

"If the last King of Bling trolley dash was an hour ago," said Scarlet, "how long will it be before the next one?"

Cedric's fingers whizzed on the abacus beads. "Twenty tills, fifteen people per till per hour ..." he said, working out the sum. "Two hours and twenty minutes," he finished.

"In two hours and twenty minutes," Scarlet said, "we will find Captain Curl in a queue at the Loony Doubloon, ready for the next trolley dash. We need to get him out of the queue, take his place, win the dash and give the treasure to the Bottle Islanders instead of returning it to the shelves. That way, we beat Gilbert Gauntlet and help the islanders in one go. Then we can go and find the last puzzle piece."

"Will there be swords?" Cedric asked. "Granny's riddle—"

"I *know* what Granny's riddle says," Scarlet said a bit testily. "Wave the sword, blah, blah."

"Show me a sword and I'll give that vile vol-au-vent a tickling he'll never forget!" One-Eyed Scott declared.

"Yippee!" Grandpa Jack shouted.

"We'll worry about the swords later," Scarlet said. "Just ... not yet."

"But Scarlet," began Melvin.

"*Not yet*, Dad," Scarlet said. "Trust me."

As a pirate captain, Scarlet knew it was important to stay calm and sound like she knew what she was doing. But deep down, she did wonder if ignoring the bit about swords in Granny's riddle was maybe a bit stupid.

What if Captain Curl was armed?

One and a half hours later, a peculiar-looking group of pirates sidled into the Loony Doubloon. They glanced up and down the aisles. No sign of Captain Curl. No sign of Gilbert Gauntlet. The coast was clear.

Scarlet pushed up her grey wig from where it had slipped down over one ear. "You're looking good, crew," she said. "Thank goodness Mitzy was able to row us back to *55 Ocean Drive* to fetch some disguises. Everyone OK?"

"Aye aye, captain," said Lila, adjusting her long red moustache.

"Ready when you are, Scarlet," Melvin said, fluffing up the feather on his large hat. Ralph lay draped around the shoulders of Melvin's coat, pretending to be a fur collar.

One-Eyed Scott and Grandpa Jack were too busy giggling at each other's outfits to answer Scarlet's question. Scarlet peered inside the buggy that One-Eyed Scott was pushing. "OK in there?" she checked.

"Why am *I* the baby?"

Cedric grumbled. His new 'toy' birds Bluebeard and Lipstick had been bribed with banana chips to stay completely still.

"Quit grumbling," Scarlet said. "We can't risk Captain Curl or Gilbert Gauntlet recognising us. This is too important." She adjusted her hat. "Mum and Grandpa Jack – you take the Cabin Furnishings section. One-Eyed Scott and Cedric – head for Pampered Pets. Dad and I'll do Treasured Toys.

We have to find Captain Curl before he gets to the tills and then make the switch at the last minute."

"So what's that lurid louse going to be disguised as this time?" asked One-Eyed Scott.

Scarlet gasped. She'd forgotten that they weren't the only ones who would be wearing disguises! How were they going to recognise Captain Curl?

"Look for wigs," Cedric suggested. "You can *always* tell."

"Clever little Niffy Knickers," One-Eyed Scott sniggered, sticking out a finger and tickling Cedric under the chin. "Ow," he added as Cedric bit him.

Everyone set off across the superstore. Scarlet's heart was thumping. If they didn't recognise Captain Curl in time, her whole Plan would be a disaster. Not for the first time on this voyage, Scarlet wished that her granny was here. Long Joan Silver would know exactly what to do in a situation like this.

"Long Joan Silver, as I live and breathe!"

Scarlet swung around to a burly old pirate standing behind her in a Loony Doubloon employee T-shirt. The pirate's face fell. "Sorry, missis," he said, backing away. "You looked a bit like a favourite old customer of mine. My mistake."

"You always did remind me of Long Joan, Scarlet," said Melvin as the pirate returned to stacking his shelf, shaking his head like a dog with water in its ears. "Now with the grey wig and everything ..." He thought of something. "Hey! If that old guy knew Joan, that means she definitely came to Bottle Island – and the last piece of the puzzle could be *right under our noses*!"

And we might have to start waving swords, Scarlet thought nervously to herself. "Don't worry about that yet, Dad," she said out loud, hurrying along the

Treasured Toys aisle and staring hard at any Loony Doubloon customers with unusual-looking hair. “Let’s find Captain Curl first.”

There were no clocks in the Loony Doubloon. Scarlet guessed that at least half an hour had passed. Spotting an unlikely hairdo, Scarlet grabbed it – and got chased down the Pirate DVD aisle by an angry woman. Twenty minutes to go, and not a sniff of Captain Curl *anywhere*.

Twenty minutes later, Scarlet and Melvin gave up. They were joined at the

tills by Lila, Grandpa Jack, One-Eyed Scott and Cedric, now holding tightly on to Bluebeard and Lipstick. Everyone looked fed up. Lipstick's eyes swivelled towards a nearby rack of parrot snacks. His beak twitched.

"Now what?" said Cedric.

"I don't know, Cedric," Scarlet said honestly. She was totally stumped.

Lila put her hand in her pocket and pulled out a bag of banana chips. She offered them around in consolation.

It was too much for the hungry parrot in Cedric's buggy.

"MINE!" screeched Lipstick. He flew up and snatched a banana chip from Lila's hand. In the flurry, Lila's moustache dropped off.

At the next-door till, a female pirate

with long blonde hair looked across at the noise. Scarlet saw the bottle of hair product in her hand. *Buccaneer Brunette.*

A blonde pirate, buying brunette hair conditioner?

The feather boa wrapped around the lower half of the blonde's face fell away, revealing a luxurious set of whiskers.

"YOU!" roared Captain Curl, dropping the bottle of Buccaneer Brunette and pointing straight at Lila. "You're the girly's mother! I'd know you and your smelly parrot anywhere!"

Wig, 'Tache and Trolley Dash

Lila stuck her moustache back on and raced away down the Goblets 'n' Flagons aisle. Captain Curl kicked off a large pair of high-heeled shoes and gave chase.

"Take Curl's place in that queue, Scarlet!" Melvin shouted. "He hasn't seen you. We'll go and help your mother!"

Scarlet ran to the next-door till and thrust a packet of parrot snacks at the checkout pirate. CHING. The till rang up a tiny gold and purple flag. *The Yo-Ho Hoedown* burst across the speakers. Scarlet whooped and punched the air. They'd done it!

"Nice outfit, Curl," the checkout pirate whispered, scratching his armpit. "Hardly recognise you."

"CongratulAAAAAYtions to our new King of Bling!" came the booming voice over the speakers. "The King of Bling trolley dash is YOURS! You have one minute!"

Scarlet seized a nearby trolley and tore through the cheering crowd. The closest aisle was Treasured Toys. Emerald aliens and silver

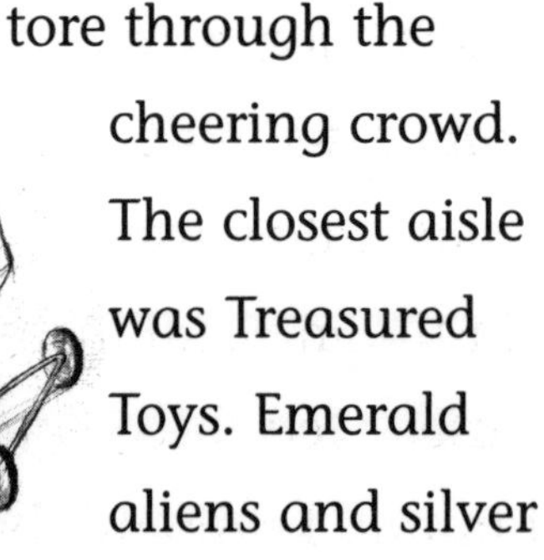

frogs, diamond dice, ruby-studded skateboards, jewel-buttoned teddies with sapphire eyes, blue-handled toy swords with pearl edges, engraved silver water pistols.

The voice on the speakers was booming out the seconds. "Thirty-three! Thirty-two! Thirty-one!"

Scarlet scooped a bucketful of Precious Pick 'n' Mix and swerved into Pampered Pets. Gold hamster wheels. Platinum cat bowls. Diamond-studded parrot collars.

"Fifteen! Fourteen! Thirteen!"

In the musical instrument section, Scarlet eyed the golden piano with the diamond keyboard, but it was just too big. She sprinted on. Tambourines edged with silver bells. Solid gold flutes. An accordion inlaid with ebony and silver. Everything went into her trolley.

"Go Scarlet!" Grandpa Jack cheered.

"Run like a shark's after yer rump!" bellowed One-Eyed Scott.

"Five! Four! Three!"

Lila appeared. "I lost Curl!" she shouted. "Let's skedaddle!"

"ONE!"

Scarlet raced through the swing doors of the Loony Doubloon and kept running, straight for the bus stop. The others followed.

"Hook it on the back!" shouted the spotty pirate at the wheel of the bus.

The Silvers hooked the trolley on the back and leaped aboard. And in a flurry of dust, the Loony Doubloon shuttle bus zoomed away from the superstore.

The treasure traders in Port Label couldn't believe their eyes as Scarlet and her family walked among their stalls, giving out the treasure they'd won at the Loony Doubloon. From being the most miserable islanders in the Seven Seas, they were now among the happiest.

"I'll have to call meself Diamond Diane now," Rhinestone Rhondda gasped as Scarlet poured handfuls of glittering gems on to her table.

When they reached Fritz the Glitz however, the Silvers got a surprise.

"Me 'n' Mitz is moving out of the treasure business for good," said Fritz. He was covered in sawdust and holding a chisel.

"Remember them vehicles and vermin traps my Fritzy makes?" Mitzy beamed.

Scarlet remembered Fritz's hobby. She nodded, interested.

"He loved making your boat so much, he's decided to set up in vehicle construction and pest control," Mitzy said proudly. "And ever since you gave us all them fish, I'm doing catering." She offered Scarlet a plate. "Flying Fish Fritter?" she said.

Wherever you get a gathering of happy pirates, music isn't far off. The Port Labellers pulled out trombones, fiddles and a couple of kazoos and launched into a merry version of *The Yo-Ho Hoedown*. Soon, the townsfolk were eating Mitzy's flying fish fritters, making up rude jokes about Gilbert Gauntlet and dancing on the beach.

Lila unzipped the waterproof casing around her accordion, ready to join in. Then she gasped. The waterproof casing wasn't waterproof after all.

"It's ruined!" Lila wailed.

Scarlet dug down into the almost empty trolley and pulled out the ebony and silver accordion. "Looks like you'll just have to play this one, Mum," she grinned.

"I WANT MY TREASURE BACK!"

Gilbert Gauntlet stood on the harbour wall with an army of henchmen. The Silvers and One-Eyed Scott automatically checked their hats, wigs and moustaches. They had to stay anonymous, or the pirate would spot them like Lipstick spotted banana chips.

Gilbert Gauntlet's glare would have made a crocodile sweat. His henchmen threw themselves at the Port Labellers in a long line of purple and gold T-shirts. The Battle of Bottle Island had begun.

A flying fish fritter flew towards Gilbert Gauntlet and knocked his hat off. Tambourines whizzed like tinkling frisbees. Trombones and fists and feet whirled and crashed and bashed. But – *no swords*. Scarlet felt both relieved and confused. Why did Granny's riddle mention swords if there weren't going to be any?

She looked down at her almost-empty trolley. The blue-handled toy swords stared up at her, their pearl edges gleaming in the light. She seized them and flung them towards her family. "Use these!" she yelled.

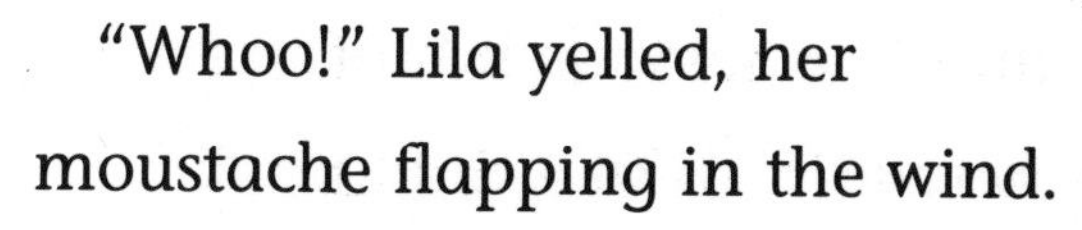

As proper weapons, the pearl-edged swords were useless. But waved about in the air, they looked *great*.

"Whoo!" Lila yelled, her moustache flapping in the wind.

"Yeah!" Cedric shouted. He attached two extra swords to his leg splints, and went whirling down the beach. Sand flew everywhere.

"Take that, you mincing meerkat!" One-Eyed Scott yelled, poking a henchman in the belly.

"Steady on, madam!" the henchman protested, looking rather shocked.

Scarlet's wig slid over one ear. She was about to push it back when—

"I've got you!" screeched a familiar high-pitched voice.

Captain Curl was pointing a finger at Scarlet as he moved towards her through the swirling sand. His bald head shone underneath his comb-over. He looked slightly mad. "I knew you'd be behind this!" he shouted. "Gilbert didn't believe me! Where's their ship? he says. Where's your proof, Curl? he says. Where's my treasure, Curl, and why did you miss that trolley dash? he says. You've ruined my reputation, and that calls for *revenge*!"

Scarlet shoved her wig back on. She whirled her sword above her head, doing her kung fu arms at the same time. "Yargh!" she cried.

Captain Curl faltered, eyeing the sword in Scarlet's hand.

"Try me, Snooker Ball Bonce," Scarlet hissed.

"I ... am ... not ... *bald*!" Captain Curl howled.

Scarlet whirled her sword again.

"I ..." spluttered Captain Curl. "You ..." And he turned and ran away as fast as he could.

Scarlet could see purple and gold T-shirts all around her in the billowing sand. Gilbert Gauntlet's henchmen were pushing the traders back.

"It's no good," Lila gasped, grabbing Scarlet by the sleeve. "Gauntlet's won the battle. We have to hide!"

Gilbert Gauntlet was doing a little dance as the Port Labellers were rounded up and hustled towards the edge of the harbour. Three of his henchmen were moving along the market stalls and taking back all the treasure Scarlet had got from the Loony Doubloon.

"They can all walk the plank," Gilbert Gauntlet shouted.

"He still hasn't seen us," Melvin

panted. “He didn’t believe Curl about Lila in the superstore, and our disguises held up pretty well.”

“I know,” said Scarlet, thrusting her pearl-edged sword into her belt. “But—”

“There’s nothing we can do, Scarlet,” said One-Eyed Scott.

Reluctantly, Scarlet let the others drag her into the nearest house. They peered through the shutters at the scene outside. The Port Labellers were shuffling along a short plank extending over the harbour. One by one they dropped off the end with a shriek, into the cold water below.

“The Loony Doubloon is here to stay,” Gilbert Gauntlet snarled over the harbour wall as the miserable treasure traders waded ashore to wring out their socks. “I’m the shark and you’re my prey.”

"That rhymes, boss," said Captain Curl in a schmoozy voice.

"I *know,*" Gilbert Gauntlet snapped. He clicked his fingers at his henchmen. "Desmond? Derek? Duncan? Doris? The rest of you? Let's go."

"Me too, sir?" said Captain Curl, looking pathetic.

"I suppose so," Gilbert Gauntlet said sourly. *"I fought Scarlet Silver, sir,"* he mimicked, striding away from the harbour with Captain Curl close on his tail as Scarlet and her family peeped out from their hiding place. *"I chased the girly's mother and Powderpuff her parrot, sir.* Impossible rubbish. Trying to impress me, eh? Get back in my good books? You are on thin ice, Dingbat. And don't you forget it."

Rich at Last

"Dingbat!" Melvin was still chortling about Gilbert Gauntlet's new nickname for his chief henchman an hour later.

"This is no time for laughter, Dad," Scarlet said. She batted Lipstick away. He'd developed an annoying habit of perching on her belt. "We've still got to pay that swaggering swine back for dunking everyone in the sea today."

The Port Labellers were looking

miserable again. Not to mention wet.

"Gauntlet's won," Fritz the Glitz muttered. "And once that massive treasure shipment comes in, he'll be unbeatable."

"What massive shipment?" asked Grandpa Jack.

"The *Golden Gosling* comes in tomorrow," explained Rhinestone Rhondda. "She's the biggest merchant ship on the Seven Seas. Gauntlet will buy the lot, and we'll be left with nothing to trade but seagull droppings."

"Why doesn't Gauntlet get his treasure delivered straight to the Loony Doubloon?" Melvin asked.

"Currents is too treacherous round the Bottleneck," Fritz the Glitz explained.

Cedric frowned. "So why didn't he

build the Loony Doubloon in Port Label in the first place?"

"Too hilly," said Mitzy.

Scarlet was struck by an idea. "There's only one road from the Loony Doubloon to Port Label, right?" she checked.

The treasure traders nodded.

"So why don't we block it?" Scarlet said.

"He'd just go round the blockage," said Rhinestone Rhondda.

Scarlet spread her arms. "So let's think big," she said. "The Bottleneck is narrow. Why don't we dig a huge trench across it and cut off the Loony Doubloon completely?"

"The sea would get into the trench," Lila pointed out.

"Exactly!" Scarlet grinned. "We can turn the Bottleneck into Bottleneck *Island*!"

"So Gauntlet can't get to Port Label for the treasure shipment!" Melvin said.

"He'll be marooned!" Grandpa Jack cheered.

"Blibbering barnacles, Scarlet," said One-Eyed Scott. "When you sez think big, you *means* big."

"I got the perfect thing!" shouted Fritz the Glitz.

Everyone goggled as the trader leaped to his feet and rushed off behind his house. There was a puttering sound and the smell of petrol. Carved and polished like the driftwood chair and the Silvers' new dinghy, an incredible machine came spluttering towards them with Fritz the Glitz riding on the top.

"Please tell me that's not a vermin trap," said Lila.

"One of the vehicles I bin constructin'," Fritz the Glitz said proudly, patting the enormous contraption. "Bit of wood, couple of nails, bit of varnish, pukka. You want a trench? Let's go dig a trench!"

They headed for the Bottleneck in the moonlight. Leading the way was Fritz the Glitz on his digging machine. People joined them every step of the way. They brought spades, forks and pickaxes. They brought rakes, coal shovels and spoons. *Everyone* wanted to dig.

"At this rate we'll be done by midnight!" said Cedric, strapping his digging implements to his leg splints and setting the speed dial to "full".

The dirt started to fly. Scarlet rolled up her sleeves and shovelled alongside Cedric, Lila and Melvin. Grandpa Jack kept watch on the dark windows of the Loony Doubloon up ahead. One-Eyed

Scott launched into his Funky Eyepatch dance to keep the diggers' spirits up. Lipstick abandoned Scarlet's belt and helped Bluebeard eat all the worms. And right in the middle of it all, Fritz the Glitz and his digging machine sliced through the earth, with Ralph snoozing on the digger's warm engine.

By ten o'clock, the trench was two metres deep. By eleven, it was double that. Mitzy dished out flying fish fritters at midnight. And at a quarter to one, Fritz the Glitz breached the end of the trench with his digging machine and the sea rushed in. The Loony Doubloon was marooned on its very own island.

The Bottle Islanders cheered like mad. Then they stopped when they remembered how close they were to

Gilbert Gauntlet, sleeping peacefully in his penthouse suite just over the water.

"Let's get some sleep," Melvin yawned. "The *Golden Gosling* will be here soon."

Out of the corner of her eye, Scarlet glimpsed something sparkling. She looked at the mountain of earth piled up beside her. Reaching into the dirt with her fingers, she pulled out a lumpy piece of glimmering, pinkish metal.

"What's that?" said Lila.

Rhinestone Rhondda snatched it out of Scarlet's hand. "You've only gone and found pink gold," she breathed.

"I didn't know it came in pink," Lila said with interest.

"Treasure's in me blood," said Rhinestone Rhondda. "That's pink gold, or I'm a mushroom omelette."

Pink gold. Pink gold. Pink gold ... The word spread among the Bottle Islanders.

"It is!"

"It's pink bloomin' gold!"

"There's more!" Cedric cried, pulling another lump out of the dirt. "And more! And *more*!"

"Unbe-blunkin'-*lievable*," Grandpa Jack said, looking dazed.

Everyone jumped on to the mounds of earth and started sifting through it. More lumps and pebbles and rocks of pink gold emerged. Everything they found was loaded into the digging arm on the front of Fritz the Glitz's digging machine.

The sky behind the Loony Doubloon was lightening. Two lights flicked on in the penthouse suite above the treasure store. Gilbert Gauntlet was waking up. And on the horizon, Scarlet spied a large merchant ship in full sail, heading steadily towards them.

"The *Golden Gosling*!" she shouted. "Everyone, back to Port Label!"

The treasure traders, the Silvers and One-Eyed Scott stood on the Port Label beach as the *Golden Gosling* dropped anchor.

They were panting heavily, but they'd made it.

Enormous golden bracelets and chains dangled from the treasure merchant's wrists and neck. He looked at the Port Labellers like a gardener might look at slugs on his vegetable patch. "Where's the boss?" he asked.

"If you mean Gilbert Gauntlet," said Scarlet, "he's not coming. We're trading with you instead."

The merchant laughed so much his chains made a jingling sound. "You must be kidding," he sneered. "What you got for me? A bit of sand? A bunch of mackerel guts?"

The Port Labellers had started moving among the trunks, boxes and bags of treasure that the merchant's crew had unloaded on to the beach.

"Get your mitts off!" yelled the merchant. "You can't afford this stuff!"

"Oh, can't we?" said Rhinestone Rhondda. She pulled a rock of pink gold out of her pocket and held it up.

The merchant's eyes boggled. "That ain't ..."

"Mackerel guts?" said Cedric. "No."

The merchant reached for the pink gold. Rhinestone Rhondda held it out of his reach. The merchant whimpered like a puppy.

"Gold as pink as

a flabbergasted flamingo," said One-Eyed Scott with a grin.

"How ..." The merchant licked his lips. "Exactly how much of this stuff have you got?"

"About an island full," Scarlet said. "We just found the biggest pink gold mine on the Seven Seas."

The merchant looked like he was about to start dribbling. "I can be your sole exporter?" he said.

"Yup," said Rhinestone Rhondda. "If you drop the attitude." Her tiara gave a menacing tinkle. "We really *hates* attitude."

The merchant spat on his hand and thrust it at Rhinestone Rhondda, who pumped it hard. The Port Label treasure traders started cheering and jumping into each other's arms. A blast of the *Yo-Ho Hoedown* came thrumming down the seafront.

"Time to go, crew," said Scarlet with more than a bit of regret.

Everyone looked surprised and disappointed.

"Well, ain't *that* as annoying as a halibut with hiccups," said One-Eyed Scott bitterly.

"Things are just getting good, Scarlet," Lila said. "I want to join in the *Yo-Ho Hoedown* on my new accordion."

"We've still got to find that last puzzle piece," Scarlet reminded them. "We've waved the sword, so it must be— *Ow*!"

Lipstick had pecked Scarlet smartly in the stomach.

"What is *with* Lipstick?" Scarlet demanded. "He's driving me crackers."

Quick as a dart, Lipstick pecked at the toy sword still hanging in Scarlet's belt. There was a clunk. Something blue fell out of the handle. Bluebeard dropped out of the sky and snatched it up before it hit the ground. The budgie did a victory loop through the air and gently dropped the final puzzle piece into Scarlet's outstretched hand.

The puzzle was complete.

Weighed down with gifts, the Silvers and One-Eyed Scott launched out to sea in their sparkly new rowing boat, complete with a freshly painted pair of oars set with pink gold.

"On the 'ouse," Fritz the Glitz said. "And next time you need any vehicular construction or maintenance – not to mention pest control – you knows where to come. Right?"

The beach was lined with waving islanders as Melvin and Grandpa Jack pulled on the oars and turned the new dinghy into the cave where *55 Ocean Drive* still lay hidden. The ship was a little damp, especially the socks in the rigging, but Scarlet knew the sea breezes would dry everything by lunchtime. Four puzzle pieces. Granny's treasure was in their grasp. She could hardly believe it.

"Yo-Ho Hoedown, yippee-ai-ay, swing your hooks and shout hurray," Lila sang, dancing on the deck with her beautiful new accordion as Grandpa Jack and One-Eyed Scott dusted down the Fishomatic.

Scarlet steered the ship out of the cave and around the corner. She waved cheerfully at Gilbert Gauntlet, who was standing on the shoreline of Bottleneck Island and staring at the water which had replaced his road. He didn't wave back.

"Yo-Ho Hoedown, yippee-ai-ee," sang Lila. *"Get on down for piracy!"*